THE TERRIBLE,
Wonderful
TELLIN'
at Hog Hammock

KIM SIEGELSON

THE TERRIBLE, *Wonderful* TELLIN' at Hog Hammock

ILLUSTRATED BY ERIC VELASQUEZ

HARPERCOLLINSPUBLISHERS

In grateful acknowledgment of the Society
of Children's Book Writers and Illustrators
for a Work-In-Progress Grant given to support
the writing of this book.

KLS

Library of Congress Cataloging-in-Publication Data
Siegelson, Kim L.
  The terrible, wonderful tellin' at Hog Hammock / by Kim L. Siegelson ; illustrated by Eric
Velasquez.
    p.   cm.
  Summary: Jonas wants to keep the memory of his beloved Gullah grandfather alive by
representing his family at the traditional storytelling contest, even though he feels like a nervous
child trying to do a man's job.
  ISBN 0-06-024877-7. — ISBN 0-06-024878-5 (lib. bdg.)
  1. Gullahs—Juvenile fiction. [1. Gullahs—Fiction. 2. Grandfathers—Fiction.
3. Storytelling—Fiction. 4. Sea Islands—Fiction. 5. Afro-Americans—Fiction.]
I. Velasquez, Eric, ill. II. Title.
PZ7.S5757Or 1996   95-30005
[Fic]—dc20   CIP
                                                                AC

Typography by Al Cetta
5 6 7 8 9 10
❖

To my grandmama, Julia Kate,
who gave me her *gift fe lie,*
and for Peggy Schweers (1962-1992),
who dropped the first acorn.

CHAPTER ONE

It was hot. Sticky, skin-prickling heat hung over the Georgia coast like teakettle steam. Jonas fanned the air in front of his face with his hand. It did little to cool him off. "August heat the worse of all," Jonas's grandpa had always said, and Jonas believed it.

He plopped down on the edge of his grandparents' rickety dock and swung his bare feet. The dock jutted out into the curve of a creek off Duplin River. Duplin was just one of many rivers that crisscrossed the tide marshes on the west side of Sapelo Island.

Jonas had no memory of the dock being built. That had happened more than a dozen years ago and he had not been born yet. His grandpa had sunk the pilings, laid the boards, and driven the nails. His grandpa and he had spent many days and evenings on the old dock fishing, telling stories, or just staring out at the marsh.

Jonas rubbed his fingers over the rough boards. The old man's death, over six months earlier, still hadn't quite sunk in. Being on the dock made him feel as if his grandpa could still be somewhere close by. Jonas remembered the last thing his grandpa had said to him the morning he'd died. "Come go catch fish with me."

Jonas had almost gone fishing, but then he changed his mind. "I'll go next time, Grandpa," he'd said. "I want to go to the beach with my friend, Zeek." Later, someone found Grandpa lying down on the dock like he was sleeping with his face to the sun. He never woke up again. While Jonas was having fun with Zeek, Grandpa's heart stopped.

Jonas hadn't been able to come to the dock for a long time after the funeral. He hated the stinging in his eyes and choking feeling he got in his throat when he was here. Everything about the dock reminded him of how he'd let Grandpa down. If he'd gone fishing like Grandpa had asked, he could have been there to fetch help. Or maybe he could have said good-bye.

The only thing he could think of to do now was not think about Grandpa at all. Forget him if he could. But that was like forgetting you had a sandspur stuck in your foot. Every step you took pushed it deeper and made it hurt even more.

A light breeze stirred the heavy air. Jonas tipped his head back, hoping it would cool his face. He stripped off his T-shirt and wiggled his feet into his oldest pair of tennis shoes. They were too tight, and full of rips from the razor edges of oyster shells that clumped on the walls of the riverbanks.

He scanned the rippling sea of spearlike grass that blanketed the flat, muddy salt-marsh meadow. The rivers were muck-filled channels right now, emptied of their water by the low tide. But it was only a matter of time before the incoming ocean tide would fill them and turn the mud flats into a chest-deep swamp.

Jonas jumped off the dock to the marsh floor and began weaving through the stiff, chin-high grass. He followed a path along the river channel that he had used thousands of times in his life. He had been three years old and just big enough to drag a shrimp net the first time he had been allowed to tag along with the men into the marsh.

Thousands of pecan-sized fiddler crabs rushed ahead of his moving feet in a wave. "Out of my way!" shouted Jonas, waving his arms around.

The sudden noise startled a blue heron into flight and made Jonas jump. "Well, Mr. Skinnylegs, don't think I want to be here. I have better things to do with my Friday afternoons. Besides, I had to gather the sweetgrass last time it ran out. This was supposed to be Rikki's turn to cut a bundle!" He kicked a clump of oyster shells into the bottom of the channel.

At the end of the path, Jonas turned away from the river and zigzagged out into the reeds. He kept his eyes open for the thin green blades of sweetgrass. The clumps grew in places where fresh water collected near the marsh and beach. It seemed harder to find every time he came out. Jonas rubbed his shoulders. He felt like a Sunday-dinner roasted hen.

"We haven't had chicken in forever," thought Jonas. "Mom said she won't cook another one till Dad comes home from Brunswick." Jonas's father and uncle Micah stayed on the mainland during the summer and worked in a paper mill. Sometimes it was a month before they were able to come home on the ferry for a weekend.

Jonas finally spotted a patch of slender, golden-tipped grass. He pulled a knife from its sheath in his pocket and began cutting the stems close to the ground.

"Longer is bestest for the weavin'," his grandmother always said to him, never lifting her eyes from the coil of basket she gripped in her fingers. Nana Myma's sweetgrass baskets were prized by the tourists who visited Sapelo Island. She shaped them like large urns and great plump apples, and she wove them so tightly they could hold water.

"This is enough," said Jonas. He wound a strand of grass around the thick bundle and lifted it to his shoulder. Turning back toward the river channel, he began retracing his zigzag path through the marsh field. Up ahead, he could see a patch of grass rippling, but no breeze was blowing.

"Marsh hens!" whispered Jonas excitedly. He threw the bundle of sweetgrass down and pulled a slingshot from the back pocket of his cutoffs.

The fat brown birds were picking their way through the grass, clucking softly. Jonas followed them for a long time. Every now and then one would pluck a wriggling crab from the mud with its thin beak and swallow it whole. *Kek-kek-kek*, they called.

"Chicken for dinner!" Jonas pulled the sling back and aimed into the middle of the group. He

let a stone fly. Hens swirled up above the grass and scattered with loud cackling and wings flapping. "Missed." He shoved the slingshot back into his pocket.

Jonas walked back to the bundle of grass and picked it up, then made his way to the bank of the river. The bottom of the empty channel was quickly filling with murky water as the ocean tide surged in toward the mainland. "Have I been out here that long?" Jonas wondered. "Stupid hens!" He began to trot in the direction of the distant dock.

Salty rushes whipped against his legs. He winced and gritted his teeth. Cutoffs had seemed like a good idea to keep cool, but they gave no protection against the sharp, stiff grass. *Crunch!* went an unlucky fiddler crab beneath Jonas's shoe. "Sorry," he called back. "Now you're fish bait!"

Water soon turned the channel into a river. It spilled over the bank and onto the marsh meadow. Jonas started to worry. Water swirled over his shoe tops, and his feet were beginning to stick in the thick, gray mud. The bundle of grass bobbed faster on his shoulder as he broke into a run.

"Last turn!" he thought as he scooted around a curve in the river. The dock was nowhere in sight; just a wall of black rushes. "Oh, no!" he said, almost panicking. "I didn't think I had gone so far out."

Jonas could no longer see his path through the water, and he was afraid to stay so close to the river now. Alligators were known to swim the channels sometimes. The older boys and men claimed not to be afraid of them, but Jonas was sure they ate more than small animals and birds. The thought of those gaping, toothy jaws sent him back into the meadow.

After stumbling through what seemed like miles of grass, Jonas stopped and looked around. He felt more lost than ever. The water had crept up to his shins. Soon it would be waist high and hard to walk in. Then he remembered something his grandpa had told him. "If ever you lost in the marsh, stop youself and look at the shore. You aim for tallest tree, near that gap there. That where the dock lie." He spotted the tree and the gap on the shore and began wading in that direction.

The floor of the marsh field was becoming softer and mushier as it mixed with the water. With every step, Jonas sank almost to his knees in the gluey mess, but he kept his eyes on the tree that meant safety.

Finally he pushed through the last of the rushes and found himself a few feet away from the dock. He sloshed to its edge and threw the bundle of grass up before hoisting himself over the side. His legs were welted and red from the slashing reeds and burning salt, and his heart-beat pounded in his ears, but Jonas hardly cared. It felt good to be safe.

Jonas caught his breath and rolled onto his

belly. He stared out at the glistening marsh. Water the color of root beer lapped at the pilings. The rhythmic slap of the waves brought back the sound of his grandpa's voice chanting in Gullah, the creole language of the islanders. People on Sapelo had been speaking Gullah for more than two hundred years, but now the older people used it more than Jonas and his friends did.

His family still spoke the "old-time talk" at home, but he couldn't use it in school. His teacher, and most other people who had not been born on the coastal sea islands, did not understand the old language. They squeezed their faces up and looked puzzled, then made you repeat the words over and over.

Jonas had a Gullah name, Oree, but only his grandparents had ever called him that. "Oree," his grandpa had said. "You remember this what I tell you now. When the tide run low, know how far you go; so when the tide run high, you left safe and dry." His grandpa had made the words rhyme so that Jonas would remember them.

"Guess I remembered too late," thought Jonas as he rose to his feet and shouldered the bundle for the walk back home to Hog Hammock.

Jonas was going to be very late getting home. The sun was just a glow behind the moss-draped branches of the ancient oak trees, and tree frogs had begun to trill. He would be in trouble for sure. A good fib might help, if he could think of one.

Jonas reached a narrow footpath that led by the community graveyard. Some of the people who were buried there had been born on the west coast of Africa and had traveled to Sapelo on Spanish slave ships before the Civil War. Now Jonas's grandpa lay there with them.

The first black islanders had chosen this secluded place to bury their dead because of the denseness of the trees and bushes. Some of them believed that at death a person's soul goes to God, but the spirit stays on earth with the body. The roots of the trees and the low-hanging branches helped keep the spirits there in the woods so they couldn't roam around and do mischief.

If it had been earlier in the day, Jonas would have taken the shortcut along the path. He and Zeek did it all the time, even though they had been told by their parents to stay out. But this time the shadows and dark corners of the woods gave him a chill. He hurried past the narrow gap in the brush. If Grandpa's spirit knew he'd gotten so lost in the marsh today, it would be sure to play some trick on him.

Farther ahead, Jonas could see a kerosene lantern burning in the window of his grandmother's shanty house. "They're already eating dinner," he thought. He decided not to stop by his own house first. Every night his whole family gathered for dinner at Nana Myma's house. Of course, they all lived next to each other; the three houses were spaced evenly around a common dirt yard. The land had been in their family since the Civil War.

Jonas could hear his family's dogs snoring and snuffling under the steps. He kicked his muddy sneakers off on the sagging front porch and dropped the bundle of grass next to some unfinished baskets left by the ladies. The dogs

lifted their heads at the racket, then groaned and flopped back down.

Nana Myma's screen door squeaked as Jonas pulled it open. It snapped back fast and caught the heel of his bare foot with a bang. "Ouch!" complained Jonas loudly. "Hey, did anybody save me any dinner? I'm half starved!" He walked into the kitchen.

"We don't save no dinner for some no-count boy that goes lazin' in the marshes while the rest of us work," snapped his sister, Rikki.

"Rest you mouth!" his grandmother warned her. "Oree will explain why he take so long. Go on, Oree." All eyes turned to Jonas.

He told them about the marsh hens and how he had just managed to beat the rising tidewaters. He even threw in an alligator chase for some extra excitement. "And to get away," he told them, "I gave the gator all the hens that I killed with my slingshot. He had to stop to eat them, one by one. And," he added, "I left the sweetgrass on the porch. It didn't even get wet."

Rikki's eyes were round with the thought of escaping from a swamp gator, but Jonas's mother pulled him down into the empty seat

14

next to hers; his father's chair. She held his chin in her fingers and spoke firmly. "Jonas, you must be the most careful. You oldest here while you daddy and the other mens is at the mill. You mind what you been taught, now on." Jonas nodded his head and turned back to the dinner table.

He took a deep sip from the cool jelly jar of iced tea that his aunt Mozi had put in front of him. Then he heaped his plate with rice and island red peas cooked with smoky ham bone. He stabbed several peas onto his fork and ate them with a bite of spicy chowchow pickles. "Mmm," he sighed as he sopped pea juice and bits of pickle up with a warm slab of buttered corn bread.

"They's gon be a big tellin' Sunday evening down to Linde's place," said Aunt Mozi. A warm, bitter smell filled the tiny kitchen as she poured coffee into three thick mugs, one for each of the ladies. "First year Papa won't be there."

"Won't nobody from our family be there to tell a good tale this time with all the mens out workin' at the mill," added Jonas's mother gloomily.

For as long as Jonas could remember, Miss Linde had always hosted the island's biggest storytelling get-together. People told stories most every night for entertainment, but this tellin' was different. Each storyteller tried hard to make his story the best one told that night. Anyone who wanted to listen was invited to sit around the fire pit in Miss Linde's yard. Most of the islanders showed up. Few families on Sapelo owned a television, so a good tellin' was always welcome, and a good storyteller became a local celebrity.

Nana Myma picked up Jonas's empty plate and carried it to the counter. She cut a leftover breakfast biscuit in half and plopped it on the plate. "Seem like you grandpa tell the bestest tale most every year since I know him. He surely did have de gift fe lie!" She chuckled as she drizzled molasses syrup over Jonas's biscuit. He took the plate from her and ran his finger through the smooth brown syrup that had spilled off the biscuit.

Grandpa had been one of the best storytellers in Hog Hammock. He could tease and draw in his audience so skillfully that, by the end, everyone hung on his every word and movement. He was like a great actor in a one-man play. Not many people had the gift; a gift Nana Myma said had been passed to Jonas when his grandpa died.

That was something Jonas wasn't so sure about. Old islanders like Nana believed that talents could be left behind for someone, just like things you could touch or hold in your hand. But Jonas had not felt any different after his grandpa's death. No tales had suddenly popped into his head, and he had never tried to make one up for himself. Maybe a few fibs, but not stories like Grandpa had always told.

"Pick up you plate, Jonas," called his mother. "Come on out the porch with us." Nana Myma, Aunt Mozie, and Jonas's mother set their mugs on the wooden floor and began twisting new sweetgrass into the tight coils of the unfinished baskets. Rikki and Jonas flopped down on the steps, his biscuit plate between them. He was sure his grandmother had not taken her eyes off him since the end of dinner. "Rikki," he whispered, "why is she givin' me the eye?"

"What're you talkin' about?" She swiped a chunk of Jonas's biscuit.

Nana Myma's fingers worked swiftly and knowingly over her basket. A pattern emerged as the coils were wound one on top of the other. The same pattern had been used by every generation of her family, hundreds of years back to the West African tribe of her ancestors.

"Oree can go to the tellin' for this family," she said thoughtfully. "He do have the gift his grandpa left him." Jonas almost choked on a piece of biscuit.

"Now, Mama," said Jonas's mother. "You know they won't let no chil' stand up there at the tellin'. Tellin' is for the mens."

"She right," chimed in Aunt Mozi. "The boy too young."

"And he already have a big-'nuff head," added Rikki.

But Nana Myma had set her mind. "I'm gon talk to Miss Linde and the mens 'bout it. Tell 'em Oree can stand up for this family at the tellin' come Sunday."

CHAPTER THREE

Jonas rolled and tossed fitfully in his bed. His sheets twisted around his body like ropes that held him far away from sleep. Darkness had brought little relief from the day's heat. The air felt still and breathless. No cooling ocean breezes tickled the edges of the window curtains on this night.

Then, through the frog burps and cricket chirps outside, Jonas heard a voice. It whispered to him, "Oree, boy, you hear me now what I tell you."

Jonas opened one eye cautiously. "Grandpa?" he whispered. He thought he could see the old man in the dirt yard outside his window. He motioned to Jonas in a slow, deliberate way. Jonas could scarcely manage to shake his head no.

He watched as his grandpa began talking and dancing around the circular yard. Every now and then he crouched low or moved his hands in the air. Moonlight seemed to shine from within him. But Jonas couldn't hear anything he was saying. "What do you want? What are you telling me?" he screamed into the darkness.

Wham! Jonas's head hit the wall next to his bed hard and he woke with a start. The sound of his own voice had snatched him back from the nightmare. His sheets were drenched with sweat, and his heart hammered harder than it had when he had been caught in the marsh.

Jonas froze when he saw the open window. "There's no such thing as ghosts and spirits," he told himself. "Only the old folks believe in those things." He sat with his back propped against the wall and stared out at the yard. It was as if his grandpa had been at Linde's, telling stories like always.

The stories he told there were different from the ones he told Jonas and Zeek and Rikki when they were alone. At Linde's he told stories passed to him by his own grandpa about plantation farms and the long, dark, sickening ride under the decks of ships that had crossed the ocean from Africa.

Those old stories made Jonas feel bad. Why

had Grandpa told terrible stories like that? Who wanted to be reminded of all those things? Jonas had always liked the ones about Bruh Rabbit and Bruh Crow and Bruh Fox better; stories that made him laugh.

Thinking about his grandpa dancing around like Bruh Rabbit made him smile. Slowly he let his muscles relax and felt himself drifting into sleep. "There are no ghosts," he murmured as he put his head on his pillow and began to snore.

unlight beamed through Jonas's bedroom window and warmed his cheeks
and nose. He clinched his eyelids tighter
and pushed his face into his pillow. "Day clean,
lazy boy!" shouted his mother outside his window. "You gon sleep this day away. Now get
youself up!"

Jonas moaned and pushed himself up on the
side of the bed. "I'm up, I'm up," he muttered.
He pulled on his shorts and shuffled into the
kitchen. He filled a bowl with the hominy grits
his mother had left simmering in a battered old
cook pot on the stove. The pot was dented so
badly that it tipped to one side.

"May not be pretty," his mother often said,
"but it do what it sposed to."

Jonas banged the pot with his spoon. "At
least one of us can do what he's supposed to."

He swirled a chunk of butter into the thick, steamy cereal in his bowl and ate standing next to the kitchen window.

His mother was sweeping the dirt yard clean like she did every morning. The chickens pecked for bugs in the dry grass around the edge. Rikki was busy carrying pails of water from the pump to the big metal tub on the porch behind Nana Myma's house. It would soak up sunshine all day, and by evening it would be just the right temperature for a refreshing bath.

Nana's house was the oldest of the three. It had been built over one hundred years ago, so it had no indoor running water. Jonas's father had offered to build her a new one, but Nana Myma had firmly told him no. "This house been standin' since before I was a baby girl," she explained. "The breaths of my parents and my husband and chilrens keep the walls standin', hold the roof up. This a livin' house. Why I want some new house with dead air inside? Liable to fall down round me while I sleep."

Jonas put his bowl in the sink and walked across the yard to his mother. His feet left perfect prints in the dirt that had been brushed smooth by her broom. "I told Zeek I would meet him on the dock while the tide's going out this morning. We're going to go shrimping," he said, half pleading. "Do you think Dad would mind if I took his new net? Mine's got holes in it."

His mother leaned on her broom and studied his face. "You can use you daddy's net, but mind you take care of it. Bring back enough shrimps and we fix up some gumbo for supper."

Before she could warn him to be careful, Jonas made a new trail of footprints back across the yard to the house. He grabbed a foam bucket to put the shrimp in, his knife, and his slingshot, and took his father's net from his parents' room. From under his bed he pulled the torn old sneakers and his lucky charm.

The charm was an old Spanish coin that his grandpa had found on the beach once after a terrible storm. He told Jonas that it had the power to draw shrimp into the net. Jonas had never gone shrimping without it, and he had never come back empty-handed.

Jonas had meant to bury the coin with his grandpa, but he'd changed his mind at the last minute. It was something special that he could carry with him and touch when the sadness pushed behind his eyes and stabbed like a blade inside his chest. The coin was a shield.

When Jonas turned the corner onto the path that led from the road to the marsh, he could see Zeek was already waiting on the old weathered dock. He had the same tight, dark curls and deep-brown complexion as Jonas, but Zeek was a head shorter and his eyes were the surprising color of pale-green ocean water. "I thought you might have forgot," he called out to Jonas. "Hurry up! The tide's been going out for almost five minutes. Those shrimp are running."

Jonas tossed his gear down on the dock and pulled on his mud-caked sneakers. "Beat you to the clearing!" he called as he grabbed up the bucket and his father's net, then ran along the bluff and away from the dock. Zeek scooted after him, and they both reached their favorite shrimping spot at the same time. The little outcropping of dry land had long been packed firm and bare by the constant trampling of their feet. It jutted into the tide river much like the dock, but farther out, with deep water on both sides.

Jonas and Zeek stood back-to-back, each choosing his favorite side of the point to throw his net. The nets were large and circular and had a long piece of cord that wove in and out of the

holes from the middle and along the edge. At the end of the cord was a loop that each boy attached to his wrist.

To catch the shrimp, you had to fling the net out over the water with a spinning motion. When it sank just a few feet below the surface of the water, you yanked the cord hard. It closed like a drawstring purse, with the shrimp caught inside.

Zeek sailed his net out over the water first. It rose high in the air and then plunged into the water with a *swoosh*. After a few seconds he pulled the cord with both hands and hauled in the first catch of the day. "Woo-hoo!" he shouted. "This river is brimming with shrimps today."

He loosened the drawstring and dumped the ghostly-pale shrimp onto the ground. Their black beady eyes stared up at the boys, and a few tried to flip away through the dirt.

Zeek jabbed his thumb on the sharp front horn of one of the largest shrimp. "Yow!" he cried, and sucked the punctured finger in his mouth. "How are you doing over there?" he asked Jonas, who was making his second cast.

"Not great," Jonas answered. "All I got so far is a mullet and some rotten weeds. I think all the shrimp are on your side today."

They watched Jonas's net sink into the dark water. He yanked the cord and pulled the net onto the bank. When he dumped it onto the ground, just a few puny shrimp dropped out. "These are hardly worth peeling," he grumbled, and tossed them into his bucket.

"You need to let your net sink more," said Zeek. "You're in too big a hurry. Something wrong?"

Jonas pulled some small fish from his net and chucked them back into the water. He tried to hurry, hating to see them gasping for air, their tiny round mouths opening and closing, desperate for the safety of the water. That's how he felt every time he thought about Sunday; like he would suffocate.

"My grandmother is going to make me stand up at the tellin' at Linde's on Sunday. I'm supposed to tell a story."

Zeek looked stricken. "How can you do that?" he sputtered. "Kids don't tell stories, they just listen. Do you even know any stories?"

Jonas flung his net far out over the water.

"They think I have Grandpa's gift. I don't know how to tell them that the gift never made it to me when he died." Jonas rubbed the coin in his pocket. "Grandpa never taught me about telling stories."

"I'm glad I'm not you," said Zeek, shaking his head, "but you can bet I won't miss this tellin'."

Jonas pulled the cord attached to his wrist and dragged the shrimp net toward the land. It was heavy as he lugged it up onto the bank. "Wow!" he shouted. "Look at how many are in here." Hundreds of silvery bodies were piled one on top of the other, their wispy antennae twisting between them like long orange hairs.

The boys dropped them by the handfuls into Jonas's bucket. Grandpa's coin still had that power. It worked in the marsh and it worked against the memories. "Will it work on other things too?" Jonas wondered to himself. He rubbed the coin again and threw his net out over the water. Another big haul.

Jonas and Zeek stopped casting when the water dropped low enough to see the tops of the oysters poking up along the low-tide mark in the riverbank. The sharp shells could slice through the thin weave of the nets like razor blades. That was why Jonas's net had holes in it. The boys picked up their buckets brimming with shrimp, threw the nets over their shoulders, and walked back to the dock.

"If you want to practice a story on me, you can," Zeek offered. "Remember when you told Rikki that story about how Soap Sally lives in the well under the pump and comes up to bite off the toes of bossy little girls? You told that one so good, she wouldn't fetch Nana Myma's water for a month!"

Jonas smiled. Rikki had been fooled pretty good with that one. He swung his feet back and forth off the end of the dock. The fiddler crabs, who had been sealed tight in their holes under the water, were beginning to pop out by the dozens as the water ebbed out into the ocean. They stared at Jonas's feet with their little popeyes.

"Soap Sally was a fib, not a story," he said, and dropped to the muddy ground below. He took his knife from its sheath and wedged a clump of oysters from the bank. "Watch out," he called, and threw them up onto the dock, then wedged off another clump. Before he had pulled himself up with the second clump, Zeek was busy opening the shells from the first one.

The oysters were closed up tight, holding water in their shells to breathe while the tide was low. When the water rose and covered them again, they would open to feed.

Jonas slipped his blade into the crease where the shells joined in the back and pried the halves apart. Inside, the soft body of the oyster lay in a few drops of water. Jonas cut through the tough muscle that connected the animal to its shell and tipped the whole thing into his mouth. It felt smooth and slippery against his tongue, kind of like the inside of his cheek, but the best part was that it tasted like the ocean and the marshes and the tides.

"We'd better get home for lunch," said Zeek as he tossed his last shell into the marsh.

"I sure don't want to be late again," agreed Jonas, pushing himself to his feet. He looked at the shell in his hand; rough and ugly on the out-side, but slick and pearly on the inside where the oyster had been. How could something be so terrible and wonderful at the same time? He shoved it into his pocket without thinking and headed after Zeek down the road to Hog Hammock.

CHAPTER FIVE

A dust cloud surrounded the boys as they walked down the unpaved road toward home. An old soda can became a soccer ball. They took turns kicking it back and forth between them up the middle of the road. Clunk, roll . . . clunk, roll.

"Want to take the shortcut?" Zeek asked. He kicked the can into the brush next to the path through the graveyard.

Jonas hesitated. He had not forgotten the night before. "I don't know, Zeek." But Zeek was already beyond the trees and halfway down the trail.

"Come on!" he yelled. "We can practice our slingshots. Grab that can."

Jonas picked up the can and followed Zeek through the trees to the clearing with its collection of grave markers and headstones. Light filtered through the branches and cast strange spotted shadows over everything. A thick layer of shiny oak leaves carpeted the ground. Short clumps of palmetto brush looked like green fans sprouting up from the ground around the bases of the tree trunks.

Most of the grave markers were tipped sideways or backward. The heavy stones had shifted and settled into the soft ground over many years. Some were so old, the names and dates had been worn away to almost nothing. And some people from long ago didn't have a marker at all. They lay still and forgotten beneath Sapelo's dark, sandy soil.

Zeek pulled a collection of old, dented cans from their hiding place inside a clump of palmetto fronds. "Who you think should have the honor today?" he asked Jonas as he swept his arm in a circle around the cemetery. "Whose stone do we line the cans on?"

Jonas dug his fingers into his side. His stomach tingled like it knew they shouldn't be there. He looked around at the possibilities. Some of the marked graves had trinkets and handcrafted ornaments on them, put there to soothe and honor the spirits of the dead. "Don't mess with any of those," Jonas said, pointing at the decorated stones. "That one either," he said, nodding toward a new headstone in the clearing. "That one's Grandpa's."

He walked over to a worn old marker covered with fuzzy black lichens and set a can on the top edge. "I think this one is my lucky stone," he said.

"We'll see about that," Zeek answered. He lined up three more cans. "I'll go first," he shouted, and ran several yards back toward the path. He drew a mark in the dirt and stood behind it.

He picked up a rock, held it in the sling while pulling back, and let it fly. *Pow!* One of the middle cans went sailing backward. *Pow!* A second one flipped to the ground. Zeek's third stone hit dirt in front of the target; his last crashed into the broad trunk of an oak tree. Zeek stepped away from the line. "Better than I did last time!" he crowed.

Jonas set the cans back up on the stone and trotted up to the mark. He loaded his slingshot and let go a rock. *Pow!* "One down," he whooped.

"Yeah, but three to go," answered Zeek.

Pow! Then again, *pow!* The third can tipped off the gravestone and landed softly in the oak leaves. "All right, already," complained Zeek, "so you beat me. Let's get going."

"Not till I've beat you real bad," Jonas teased. "Watch me get that last can."

Zeek shrugged and leaned against the rough bark of an old live oak. Jonas loaded his sling one more time. He closed one eye, aimed at the lone soda can, and pulled the thong back with all his might. *Zing!* The stone shot through the air, missed the can completely, and hit another gravestone. *Crack!*

"You hit a marker! Let's get out of here!" shouted Zeek. He grabbed up his net and bucket of shrimp and ran down the path. Jonas stood at the line, not moving. The stone had smashed right into the pale-gray front of his grandpa's marker.

Even standing several feet back, Jonas could see the ragged chip that had been knocked out of the first letter of his grandpa's name. He crept toward the grave and bent in front of the damaged marker. He dropped his slingshot and rubbed the chipped place with his finger, trying to erase it. "No use," he said to himself.

"You coming?" Zeek called anxiously from the road. "You better get out of there. Oh, man! I just hope those spirits know it was your rock and not mine that did that."

As Jonas squatted down on his heels and searched the grass for the missing chip, he felt something dig into his thigh. "The shell." He dug his hand into his pocket.

The thin light lit the pearly curve inside the oyster shell. It shone soft pink and misty green and gray. "I'm sorry," he whispered to the gravestone, and laid the shell in the leaves over his grandpa's head. Then he grabbed his bucket and net and ran out of the thicket.

CHAPTER SIX

The boys reached Jonas's house first and stopped in the front yard. Neither had said much on the way home; each had been thinking about what had happened in the graveyard.

"So, see ya later," said Zeek, kicking at a tuft of grass.

"Sure," answered Jonas. "Just don't tell anybody about the stone. Okay?"

Zeek nodded and stared at the ground. "Do you think anything will happen to us?" he whispered.

"No. Of course not. It's just a stone. Besides, there aren't any real ghosts."

Zeek nodded and headed down the road. When he reached the bend, he turned and waved at Jonas. Jonas watched him until he disappeared around the curve.

Jonas walked by his grandmother's house without looking up, hoping she wouldn't see him. Then he ran the rest of the way across the yard and up his front steps.

He kicked off his sneakers and pulled open the screen door. "Jonas," called his mother from the kitchen, "that you? I was startin' to worry."

"It's me," he answered. "We lost track of time in the marsh."

His mother leaned over the stove with a spatula in her hand. The smell of toasting bread and melting cheese made his mouth water. He hadn't realized he was so hungry. "Grilled cheese sandwiches?" he asked.

"Um-hum." She nodded and looked up at him. He hoped she wouldn't ask any more questions about where they'd been.

Jonas held the foam bucket out in front of him. "Look at all them shrimps!" she exclaimed. "Be 'bout enough gumbo feed all Hog Hammock, we cook 'em up," she teased.

She handed him a plate and one of the crisp, golden sandwiches. He sat at the table and broke the sandwich in half, letting strings of melted cheese sag down onto the plate. "Caught a mullet, too," he told her, "but I threw it back."

Jonas's mother dumped the shrimp into the sink and began to clean them for the gumbo. "You grandpa did love smoked mullet fish. Out catching 'em on the day the Lord took him home."

Jonas winced. The day he should have been there with Grandpa instead of with Zeek. Now he'd ruined Grandpa's stone, too.

"Nana on over talkin' to Linde," his mother said, looking over her shoulder. "You know what story you gon do come tomorrow?"

Jonas rolled a string of cheese back and forth beneath his finger. He shook his head no. Maybe Linde or the men would tell Nana Myma that he could not tell a story until he was older.

"You best be thinkin', then," his mother said, and turned back to the sink.

In the time it took Jonas to finish his sandwich, she had cleaned more than half of the shrimp. Without their shells to protect them, they looked a lot smaller than they had in the bucket.

"Maybe I'll go down to the beach and think about a story," he told her.

"You get you chores done before you go then, sir," she answered.

Jonas wiped his hands off on his shorts and scooted out of the house. He hung his father's net on the front porch rail to dry, then jumped down and ran to the back of the house. He carried an armful of wood to Nana Myma's house and dropped it on the back porch next to the door. She used several logs every day in an old kettle stove to cook dinner; even more in the winter, when she used it to heat the house.

Finished with that, he grabbed a fishing pole and tackle box and started out for the beach. "Hey," someone called to him from Aunt Mozie's house, "where you goin'?" It was Rikki.

"To the beach," he answered without stopping.

"Wait, I'll come with you." Rikki disappeared from the window she had been standing at.

Jonas walked faster, but Rikki ran to catch up with him. "No girls allowed," he said. She pretended not to hear him. "I won't talk to you if you come, and I'll throw you in the water," he warned her. "Now get out of here. I don't want you to come this time."

Rikki stopped and put her hands on her hips. "You think you so big. If you don't let me come with you, you'll be sorry."

Jonas turned around and laughed. "What you gonna do? Put the hoodoo on me?"

"No," she answered, "I'm gonna tell Mama 'bout you and Zeek in the graveyard and what you did to Grandpa's stone."

The smirk dissolved from Jonas's face. He didn't take another step.

Rikki could see that she had won, and skipped up beside him. "I knew you wouldn't say no if I asked you nice," she sassed.

"What were you doing, spying on us?"

Rikki shook her head. Her braids waggled from side to side. "Mama asked me to go down to Mr. Bennie's store and see if he had some okra for the gumbo. I was comin' home when I seen you and Zeek go into the cemetery. I just wanted to see what you was up to."

Jonas looked at her doubtfully. Now she would have something on him forever. If she didn't tell on him now, she probably would some other time. He let her tag along.

Rikki talked all the way to the beach, but Jonas barely heard what she said. All he could think about was the tellin' tomorrow and what he would say and whether or not Rikki would tattle on him to Nana Myma or their mother. His

head felt like it would pop from thinking so hard.

When they reached the beach, they walked out onto the powdery gray sand. It was hot as coals from the searing August sun, but Jonas and Rikki dug their toes in anyway. Leaving their feet naked most of the summer had made the soles tough and thick as the pads of old yard dogs. They barely felt the stinging heat.

Jonas sat down with his fishing pole and tied a hook onto the end of the line.

"What story you gonna tell tomorrow?" Rikki asked. "I could help you pick a good one."

He pretended not to hear her. He pushed himself to his feet with the pole and walked to the water's edge. Rikki followed along behind him.

"Don't you even know any stories to tell?" she demanded.

"No, I don't," Jonas snapped back at her, "and I don't want to think of one. I won't have to anyway. Nobody's gonna let me stand up and tell no story. And nobody can make me, either." He baited the hook with a sand flea and cast it into the waves.

Rikki stared out at the ocean. "Those stories Grandpa told at Linde's always scared me anyhow," she said. "You wouldn't tell one of those, would you?"

Jonas didn't answer her.

"But I always liked the one about how the rabbit got a white tail, and the one about the fox and the briar patch," she went on. "Remember how Grandpa danced around and hooted when the fox threw the rabbit in the briars?"

Jonas smiled. "Yeah, 'cause the rabbit had tricked the fox into letting him get away. And Grandpa could look just like a crow sittin' on a limb when he told the ones about Bruh Crow."

Rikki tried to flap around like Grandpa had, while Jonas anchored his pole in the sand. Then the two of them walked along the beach toward an inlet where one of the marsh rivers opened out into the sea. Shrimp boats dotted the line where ocean and sky met. Their huge nets dragged the seafloor from both sides of each ship. The nets churned up the water and sent seaweed and ocean trash toward the shore.

Jonas waded out into the ocean near the river and began to swim toward the channel.

"Where you goin'?" Rikki yelled. "You

know I don't like swimmin' when the water's all full of seaweed."

Jonas floated on his back and watched her. She stood on the beach for a while, then turned on her heel and stomped back to the fishing place. He watched her yank his pole out of the sand and throw it up into the dunes before she left through the trees that bordered the beach.

Jonas floated for a while with his eyes closed. Strands of seaweed tickled his back like feathers as they slipped beneath him in the water. Different stories kept weaving in and out of his mind. The more he tried to think of something else, the more they seemed to interrupt. "But I could never do it like Grandpa," he thought. He touched the pocket that held the Spanish coin, just to be sure the small, hard circle was still safely there.

Feeling himself drift with the flow of the incoming tide, Jonas stood up and waded in toward the beach. He found the spot where his pole had been and sat waiting for the waves to inch their way up to his feet. The sun had dipped behind the tallest branches of the oaks, sending striped shadows across the sand toward the water.

As the waves began to suck the sand from around his toes, Jonas had the creepy sensation that someone was watching him from the trees. "Probably Rikki spying again," he said to himself. "Come on out, Rikki!" he yelled as he looked over his shoulder.

No one answered him.

Jonas shrugged and fished his lucky coin from his pocket. Holding it between his thumb and fingers, he used a pinch of wet sand to polish it. Around and around he rubbed sand against the metal until it shone gold like the marsh rivers at sunset. It would bring him luck. He just knew it. Rikki wouldn't tell about the graveyard, and somehow he would not have to tell a story in front of everybody at Linde's.

He picked up the tackle box and began searching the dunes for his pole. Suddenly he felt the hairs on the back of his neck bristle. Someone *was* watching him.

He spun around toward the trees and dropped to his knees. He could just see a pair of shiny black eyes glint from among the limbs of one of the oaks. Jonas sat motionless, and stared back at the unblinking eyes.

CHAPTER SEVEN

After what seemed like hours, an enormous black crow flew from the oak and soared out over the ocean. Then it turned sharply and headed back toward the shore, skimmed high above the dunes, and vanished behind the tops of the trees.

Jonas had never seen a crow that large, and there were almost never crows on the beach. If he believed in ghosts, he would think the crow was a spirit playing a trick on him. Marsh crows were tricky anyway. "Bruh Crow, now he love somethin' shiny," Jonas's grandpa had told him. "Don't turn you back, 'cause sho' nuff, he take what you got." That was it. The glint of his lucky coin had probably attracted the bird, nothing more. Still, he found his pole and left the beach as quickly as he could.

Rounding the corner, Jonas looked for

Rikki. He certainly didn't want to run into her again. He slipped around the back of his grandmother's house, through the yard, and up the porch stairs as quietly as he could. He let the screen door close gently and leaned his fishing pole against the wall.

"Jonas," his mother called out, "go on over to Nana's. She got something to talk with you about."

Jonas suddenly felt like he had swallowed a fiddler crab. One that moved around in the pit of his stomach, tickling and pinching his insides.

As he walked next door, chickens scurried across the yard in front of him. He stopped at the bottom of Nana's porch steps and crossed his fingers. He hoped she would tell him that he didn't have to stand up in front of everyone and make a fool of himself. Or maybe Rikki had told her about the chip he'd made on Grandpa's stone, and that was what she wanted to talk about.

Jonas could not make himself walk up the steps. He sat on the bottom one and rubbed the head of the dog that had pushed its nose into the palm of his hand. The peppery smell of shrimp-

and-sausage gumbo drifted through the screen door. Suddenly it snapped open. "Oree!" Nana scolded him. "I been wait half this day for you. We got us something to talk about." She carried several baskets out onto the porch and dropped them next to her chair.

Jonas looked up at her. The fiddler crab climbed to his throat and sat there like a lump.

"I talk to Linde and the mens at Mr. Bennie's store this mornin'. I tell 'em about you gift and how you is gon stand up for this family," she said.

"What did they say?" he managed to squeeze past the crab.

Nana Myma's face broke into a smile that bunched the lines around her eyes and mouth into pillowy folds. "Well, first they act like it kinda funny, but they see I don't laugh. So they talk about it 'mong themselfs and decide it be all right. Tomorrow, the sun de red fe down, you gon stand up and do you grandpa proud-proud!"

Sunset tomorrow! He had exactly one day to come up with a story he could do without making a complete fool of himself in front of everyone in Hog Hammock.

The dog nudged his hand with its nose. He

had stopped moving his fingers through its fur. "Come on, boy! Let's go to the river," he called to it, running across the yard. But the dog just yawned and looked after him, then crawled back onto the cool dirt beneath the steps.

"Jonas! Stay right where you is!" his mother called out to him from the porch. He stopped just short of the road. "You not goin' to no river this time of day. It almost dark and time for supper. Get youself washed up and back to Nana's."

Jonas didn't need to eat. What he needed was to run as hard as he could and to lie on Grandpa's dock and think about the tellin'. He needed to hear the old man's voice chant with the water and whisper through the grass.

He shuffled to the pump and washed his face and hands before walking over to Nana Myma's house for dinner.

Rikki glared at him as he walked through the kitchen door. Her eyes bored into him as hard as if she'd poked him with one of her bony fingers. He looked back at her pleadingly before picking up his bowl from the table. Nana ladled the thick, stewy gumbo into his bowl over a big spoonful of rice. Jonas stirred the mixture around and around with his spoon, taking a small bite every now and then.

"Gumbo most always you favorite," his mother said. "What the matter, you got the nerves 'bout tomorrow?"

"He got nerves 'bout something!" Rikki said, and smiled at him slyly.

Jonas poked her with his big toe under the table.

"I bet he just can't think which of his grandpa's stories he gon tell." Aunt Mozie laughed. "Got so many floatin' round in his head." Jonas smiled at her weakly. He'd be lucky if he could stand up there and say his own name. Everyone would be disappointed in him, and sad that Grandpa's stories were lost. He should have listened to the stories closer. He hadn't known they'd be so important. It was another way he'd let Grandpa down, just like in the marsh.

He could feel the prick of tears begin in the corners of his eyes, and he blinked hard to push them away. He stared at the bowl of gumbo in front of him, pushing the food back and forth with the tip of his spoon until it grew cold. The coffee mugs clanked together as his mother arranged them on the counter. Jonas put his bowl in the sink and walked out to the porch to wait for them to join him with their coffee and their weaving.

He paid no attention to their chatter as they settled into the porch chairs and began to wind the supple sweetgrass into coils, pausing from time to time to sip from a cup. Rikki sat with her back to him and worked on a practice basket. Suddenly she turned toward him and smiled. "Why don't you tell us a story, Jonas?" she asked sweetly. He saw the smile on her lips, but the look in her eyes told him she was still dangerously angry at him.

"Yes," said Aunt Mozie. "Been a long time since I heard a good lie."

Jonas looked down and rubbed his hands against his legs. The fiddler crab began to do a tap dance on the gumbo in his stomach. "I . . . I can't tonight," he stammered. "I haven't practiced enough yet." Rikki snorted at him in disgust and turned back to her basket.

"Jonas want to save up for the big night," his mother said. "He got plenty time for tellin' later. We'll get Nana for tell a tale." Jonas looked up at her thankfully.

Nana Myma laid her basket in her lap and stared out into the darkness. Dogs shuffled beneath the porch, and leaves whispered in the soft evening breeze. They all waited for her cue that the story had begun.

Suddenly she stamped her foot on the floorboards and let out a cackle. "Hoo-wee!" she laughed. "Bet not a one of you remember how it is that rabbit came for get such short tail." Jonas did remember. Grandpa'd told lots of tales about tricky brother rabbit. Most stories called him Bruh Rabbit.

"Tell us 'bout it, Nana!" urged Aunt Mozie. The rest of them nodded and pleaded with her to tell them. The old woman's eyes sparkled in the light of the kerosene lantern. She looked around the circle of faces, lingering on Jonas's before beginning the tale.

"Listen up," she said, "and I tell you straight."

CHAPTER EIGHT

Nana Myma adjusted herself in her chair. She put her basket and cup on the porch floor, leaned forward, and began the story.

"Now they's all kind of rabbit in this world. Some is smarter than other, some got natural-born tricky ways 'bout 'em, but one thing for sho'; it the lazy one what get the whole bunch in trouble. Why the rabbit come to have such short tail is 'cause of one great big ol' swamp rabbit what try to outsmart the alligator down to the river one day.

"Now ol' swamp rabbit not so quick as jackrabbit or so pretty as a cottontail. He really kinda lazy and triflin', but he got plenty sense in

him head. He down to the river one day and want for cross to the other side, but can't find no bridge nowhere gon get him there. It a wide and deep river too, and he don't swim, so he got to think of something.

"He see ol' gator swimmin' round down in the water and he holler at him, 'Oh! Bruh Gator! Come on over, let me talk with you awhile.'

"Now, gators like to eat rabbit; most specially fat, slow-movin' swamp rabbit. He glide on over to the riverbank and he cock his head. 'What you want, Bruh Rabbit?' he ask him.

"Bruh Rabbit don't get too close, but he look at him sassy and say, 'I bet you it's more rabbit in the swamp than gators.'

"Bruh Gator just laugh at him. 'Harumph!' he say. 'That not so.'

"'Well, you call up all you gators and line 'em up cross this river end to end. I count 'em and find who right,' dare the rabbit. So Bruh Gator start to bellowin' and swishin' round in the water. Soon enough all them gators come round to find out what wrong. Bruh Gator, he tell 'em line up nose to tail cross the river; so they do.

"No sooner they make that line than the swamp rabbit jump from one back to another, countin' loud as he go, 'One, two, three, four,' and so on till he done reach the other bank.

"Soon as them feets reach dry land, he sets down and start cleanin' that river mud off his long, bushy white tail. While he cleanin' and soakin' the tail in the river water, Bruh Gator swim up to him and say, 'Now it your turn. I call out all the gator, so you call all the rabbit. We count 'em up and see who right.'

"Bruh Rabbit like to crack his sides, he laugh so hard. He tell the gator, 'I don't intend to call out no rabbits—I just needed for get cross this river, thank you very much!'

"Bruh Gator get powerful mad when he hear such. 'No swamp rabbit gon make a fool of me,' he thought. Quick as lightning, he throw his head round where Bruh Rabbit washin' his tail in that water and bite the end off it. From that day to this, all rabbits been made to suffer for Bruh Rabbit's no-good trickery. Swamp rabbits, jackrabbits, and the cottontail all got a short tail.

"Now my tale been told!"

And with that Nana Myma sat back in her chair, and they all laughed to think of such a thing happening. Jonas had watched his grandmother carefully. He saw how she made them want to hear the story even though they had all heard it before.

His grandpa had danced around and made himself look like the animals or people he was talking about, but Nana sat in her chair and kept her eyes on them. She swished her arms around like a big gator's tail and made her voice deep like a gator might talk or high and teasing like a rabbit. It wasn't so much the story as how you told it.

Hearing the tale gave Jonas a place to start thinking. Nana had told the story, but Jonas kept seeing Grandpa in his mind. He let himself remember the old man's voice and the warm, dusty smell of his clothes when they sat close together. It hurt to remember.

Jonas excused himself from the porch and walked home. In his bedroom he took the lucky coin from his pocket. He rubbed the smooth, warm surface between his fingers and thought hard about the story he would tell. Tonight he would decide on one, and tomorrow he would practice all day.

He leaned back against the pillows on his

bed and closed his eyes. All the characters in Grandpa's stories rolled through his head in a jumble until he drifted off. His dreams were of soft, dark feathers; stiff, black wings; and a sharp, ebony beak that held a glittering gold coin out to him. A gift. He reached as far as he could, stretching and stretching, until finally he could grasp the metal firmly in his fingers and pull it away from the bird.

CHAPTER NINE

Jonas bolted out of bed as soon as the first beam of morning sunlight cut through the crack between his bedroom curtains. His mother had left a few cold biscuits in a cloth-covered basket on the kitchen stove. Jonas grabbed one, sliced it open, and sandwiched a piece of cheese between the halves. He drank a mouthful of milk from the pitcher in the refrigerator, then headed out for the marshes.

When he reached the dock, Jonas sat cross-legged in the middle of it and ate his breakfast. This was his favorite time of day to be here. The water moved in slow, easy currents around the river curves and out to sea. Hawks swooped over the marsh looking for prey, and flocks of snowy egrets shuffled through the shallows on slender legs, stirring up food. The air felt cooler and smelled fresh—like a fish just pulled from the water. But best of all, he could watch as the sun pulled itself up from beyond the ocean and over the treetops.

He had decided on the story he would tell at Linde's. It was one of his favorites that Grandpa had told; the one about the horse and the mule. Now all he had to do was figure out how to act it out, then practice it good before evening.

He decided to start by saying the whole thing out loud, so that he could get used to hearing himself tell it. "One Sunday," he started, "Bruh Horse and Bruh Mule were turned out to pasture together."

"What're you doing?" called a voice from behind him. "You taken up talking to yourself?"

Jonas could feel the heat creep up his neck and into his cheeks. "Zeek!" he said irritably. "Don't just sneak up on a person like that. It's not funny."

Zeek flopped down on the dock. "Thought I'd find you out here. Went by your house and Rikki said she hadn't seen you all morning. Your mama said tell you to be home before church starts. By the way, that story sounds funny when you don't tell it in the old-time talk."

Jonas pursed his lips. "You know, I can't practice my story with you watching me."

"All right, then," Zeek answered, spinning around backward, "I won't watch you. I'll look the other way. You go ahead."

That hadn't been exactly what Jonas meant, but he began again. He started out softly at first, but once he got used to Zeek being there and felt sure he wouldn't forget part of the story, he stood and began to act parts of it out. He galloped around and around the dock, faster and faster, flapping his hand behind like a tail. Jonas's horse was so funny, both boys fell over laughing and almost rolled off the dock.

"You two up to some such funny business?" A deep male voice broke through their giggles.

Jonas jumped to his feet and ran toward the man. "Daddy! When did you get home? Nobody told me."

His father put his hand on Jonas's head. His clothes and skin always had the eggy smell of sulphur from the paper mill. Even his church clothes. "Shrimper give us a ride home late last night. I come in and there you was sleep, still in you clothes. Come day clean, you gone. How you, Zeek?"

"Just fine, sir," Zeek answered, looking embarrassed for being there. "See you later at the
tellin'," he said, and rose to his feet. "I best be
getting home." He waved back at Jonas before
taking the path to the road.

What a perfect day this was going to be! It
had been weeks since he had done anything
with his father. After church they could seine or
fish off the beach, or maybe go boating down
Mud River into Teakettle Creek. He was just
about to suggest they take out the boat when he
noticed how seriously his father was studying
him. "Something wrong?" Jonas asked.

His father rubbed his hand over his cheek
and stared out at the waving grass. "Just
stopped by you grandpa's grave on the way.
Seem like the marker got itself a chip. How you
think that could be?" he asked.

Jonas suddenly felt like he couldn't breath.
Rikki snitched! She couldn't keep anything to
herself even for one day. "Maybe something hit
it," Jonas answered. "What did Rikki say?"

His father turned and gave him a puzzled
look. "Why I should ask Rikki? When she start
using a slingshot?"

Jonas looked puzzled too. His father reached

into his pants pocket and pulled out the sling-shot. "Found this lyin' up near the marker with some cans scatter all round. Thought it looked like yours or Zeek's."

Jonas realized he hadn't seen his slingshot since they had run out of the graveyard, and they sure hadn't taken the time to clean up the cans. Rikki was no snitch; he'd told on himself.

"It wasn't Zeek's fault; that one's mine," he admitted, looking away from his father. "What are you going to do?" He could feel his father's eyes studying him. Jonas concentrated on watching his foot swing back and forth over the water beneath the dock.

"First off," his father began, "you don't get the slingshot back till you can show you big enough to be responsible. Next, I'm gon talk to Zeek daddy and you two is gon clean up that graveyard. Not only you own mess, but movin' limbs, sweepin' leaves, and cuttin' weeds from the path." Jonas looked up miserably and nod-ded his head. "And last, you gon come on home right now and tell Nana about what happened."

Jonas cringed. That was the one thing that he didn't want to have to do. He followed his dad back to the road. The walk home seemed so long. Prisoners being led to their cells for the first time must feel like this, he thought. Like a rock's been tied around your neck to pull you over and make you tired.

As soon as he could see the yard, Jonas felt like every step he took was in slow motion. "Go on over and talk to Nana," his dad said.

"Can't we wait till after church?" Jonas pleaded. "Or after the tellin'?"

"You be a lucky man to go to the tellin' at all, sir," his father answered. The look on his face sent Jonas moving toward the blue-painted screen door of his grandmother's house.

He found Nana on the back porch steps plucking feathers from the breast of one of the yard hens. Another lay bare and headless in a plastic dishpan on the step below where she sat. Feathers swirled around her feet and across the backyard like soft brown leaves. He knew they must be cooking up a big Sunday lunch for his father and his uncle Micah.

Nana Myma looked up from the chicken in her hands and motioned for Jonas to take a seat on the steps. "Got somethin' for talk 'bout with you, Oree," she told him. He rested his elbows on his knees and buried his chin in his cupped

hands. Maybe she already knew. He braced himself for the scolding she would give him, and for her disappointment in him.

"Oree," she began, "you mama tell me you been worry 'bout the tellin'. She think maybe you not ready to stand up like you grandpa." This was not what Jonas had expected. He didn't know what to say.

Before he could think of something, Nana patted his leg and shook her head for him not to interrupt her. "You daddy and Uncle Micah home now, and they tell me it not right to make a chil' worry 'bout doing something 'fore they ready. Nana don't mean for you be worryin' youself sick. You daddy gon stand up at Linde's and tell the tale now. No more worry."

Jonas could feel tears well up in his eyes, stinging them under his eyelids. Nana Myma was apologizing to him! He wondered if a person could choke on misery. He hadn't even realized how much he wanted to be the one to tell a story like Grandpa at Linde's until now. He wanted to remember the stories, and he wanted to remember Grandpa. Most of all, he wanted to make up for not being there that day in the marsh. Maybe then the dreams and ghosts and sadness would leave.

He rubbed his toes in the silky, curled feathers on the steps for a few minutes until he could speak clearly. Nana was right. His father or Uncle Micah should be the one to stand up, not him. But knowing that didn't help the way he felt. And he still had to tell her about the stone. "Nana," he finally blurted out, "Zeek and me were playing in the graveyard, and I chipped Grandpa's marker."

His grandmother's hands stopped their work. She turned away from him without a word, but the look he had seen on her face brought the tears rushing back. They pushed in his throat and chest and eyes like the ocean against the stones of a jetty. This time he let them spill, hot and salty, onto his cheeks, and he didn't care if everyone saw them.

CHAPTER TEN

Jonas and Zeek worked together silently. Jonas wove between the markers picking up sticks and limbs and laying them in a neat pile at the back edge of the graveyard while Zeek swept leaves and trash with a rake. They were careful not to disturb the decorations and gifts left on a few of the graves.

Jonas noticed the oyster shell was still lying where he had left it on Grandpa's grave. He pressed it farther into the dirt with his hand. Then Jonas picked up the handle of the scythe and walked to the path. He swung it back and forth in an arc in front of him, cutting the weeds down to short stubble.

"Hey," shouted Zeek, "aren't you ready for a break?"

Jonas dropped the scythe and ran his hands over his sweaty face. "Yeah," he answered, glad that his friend had spoken first.

They sat leaning against the trunk of the largest tree in the cemetery. Its bottom branches just touched the top of Jonas's head and reached out in all directions, providing a cool, mossy shade. Zeek unscrewed the lid from a plastic jar of water Jonas's mother had sent with them, and drank deeply. He wiped his mouth on his forearm and passed the jar to Jonas.

"Daddy took my slingshot," he said. "Can't believe you left yours right on your grandpa's grave!" Just then an acorn landed on Zeek's bare shoulder. "Ouch!" He rubbed the spot where the pointy end had struck.

Jonas laughed, spewing water through his nose. Another acorn fell between them, and another one landed on Zeek. Finally one hit Jonas right on the ear. "Hey," he shouted, jumping up. "What's going on? Someone's dropping those on purpose."

The boys walked around and around the tree, trying to see through the thick leaves. They could hear something rustling among the branches. A few more acorns fell to the ground where they had been sitting. Zeek backed up into the clearing to get a better view. "What do you think of this?" he shouted at Jonas. "It's a big old marsh crow who's bombing us with those acorns!"

Jonas walked over to Zeek. Could it be the same crow from the beach? Was it following him? He looked over at his grandpa's grave and shivered. He didn't have his lucky coin with him this time.

The crow peered at them from the leaves and ruffled its feathers. It bent down and wiped the sides of its beak back and forth against a branch the way you sharpen a knife on a whetstone. Then it looked directly at Jonas. It held his gaze for several moments before flapping off toward the marsh.

"Let's hurry up and finish," Jonas urged Zeek. He picked up the scythe and swung it as fast as he could. Weeds flew wildly in all directions. When the clearing finally looked neat and the cut weeds had been raked away, the boys picked up the tools and the jar and headed back to Jonas's house.

Just like she had promised, Jonas's mother had left two plates of lunch in the oven. He and Zeek took them to the kitchen table and quickly began to devour the food that was heaped on them.

Tall, airy biscuits; lima beans cooked with butter and pepper; fresh sliced tomatoes that tasted like sunshine; pieces of okra rolled in cornmeal and fried crisp in bacon drippings; and sweetly sour cucumber pickles. But best of all, after a month of waiting, was Jonas's mother's special fried chicken. The boys savored each crunchy, juicy bite like it was the last meal either would ever eat.

"What a feast!" joked Zeek, rubbing his rounded stomach.

"Yeah," agreed Jonas, "working hard can sure make you hungry."

"You still going to tell that horse story tonight at Linde's?" Zeek asked. He put his empty dish in the sink.

Jonas drew his lips into a tight line and shook his head. "Nope," he answered. "Daddy's home, so I guess he'll be tellin' a story instead. Nana told me so this morning."

"What luck!" shouted Zeek, and clapped Jonas's back. "I bet you're happy about that. I sure would be."

Jonas nodded and gave Zeek a halfhearted smile. "I guess I'm lucky."

He didn't feel lucky though, not lucky at all.

He had ruined his grandpa's stone, made his father mad, and disappointed Nana, and he wouldn't be able to show how he remembered the stories. How maybe he did have the gift.

He would not know it himself unless he stood up that night at Linde's.

CHAPTER ELEVEN

Evening turned out perfect for a good
tellin'. It was dry, with a sweet breeze
blowing in like salt taffy from the
ocean side of the island. The moon was a thin
white sliver surrounded by pinpoint stars.
Jonas's whole family walked together over to
Linde's place.

Rikki jabbered on like always, talking about
everything and nothing at all. Jonas was re-
lieved that she hadn't said two words to him
since he'd gotten in trouble. She just kept giv-
ing him smug sideways looks that said *nah,
nah*. Everyone seemed to be in a good mood,
laughing and catching up on what had happened
over the last month. Everyone but him.

He straggled behind the group, worrying
about what he would do at Linde's. He hadn't
had the nerve to talk to his father about it. Not

even when his dad had praised Jonas and Zeek for the way they had cleaned up the graveyard. "A fine job, fe true," he'd said. "You can go with us to Linde's, come night."

Jonas put his hand in his pocket and found the circle of warm metal there. He traced the edge with his thumb while he thought.

When they got nearer to Linde's, Jonas could see the sparks from the fire pit flying up over the trees that surrounded her house. The yard was packed with people. It looked like most of Hog Hammock had already arrived. Linde was tending to two big washtubs full of stew called low-country boil. The tubs rested a little unsteadily on two beams over the fire.

Everybody who came brought something to put in the stew, and Jonas's mother and Aunt Mozi added a dozen ears of shucked corn to the simmering broth full of whole potatoes, shrimp, sausage, onions, blue crabs, and hot peppers.

Jonas could see dozens of fat sweet potatoes shoved into the coals of the fire beneath the pots. Once you peeled away the sooty skin, you found the sticky, caramel-flavored meat of the potato waiting inside.

"Glad for see you made it home for the

tellin'," Miss Linde said to Jonas's father. "Guess we won't be hearin' from the boy this time."

His father laughed. "No, I be the one tellin' it this year. Jonas near eat hisself up for worryin' he have to do it. So sick with it he couldn't eat gumbo!" Then he added, "Won't be the same now the old man bury."

"Sho' won't," agreed Miss Linde, stirring the new corn down into the stew pot.

Jonas wandered through the crowd, looking for Zeek. He hoped his friend had been allowed to come after the trouble they'd gotten into. He saw Rikki sitting with a group of her friends from school, so he turned around and headed back toward his parents. Everyone had gathered into a circle around the middle of the yard, still talking, but waiting for someone to get up and start the tellin'.

Mr. Bennie stood and drifted in toward the center. He waved to someone across the circle and shook a few hands before he sat on a log that had been pushed into the yard.

Everyone got quiet and he began his story. Jonas watched him closely, more closely than he ever had at a tellin' before. He listened to the story the old man told of life on Spaulding Plantation. Of laboring in the fields of Sea Island cotton and sugarcane. And of the summer sickness that took many lives.

Jonas had seen the old plantation house many times. It still stood solid on the south end of Sapelo, a witness to the past. Nana's and Grandpa's parents had worked and lived there.

He thought about Grandpa's stories. The folks in them were not characters. They'd been real people; people worth remembering. Those same people lay beneath the crooked black-and-gray stones of the cemetery, just like Grandpa. Grandpa hadn't told the old stories to make people scared or sad. He'd told them because they were about him and everyone here, and if they didn't remember them to each other, nobody else would. They would vanish like the names worn smooth from the oldest markers in the cemetery. They were terrible and wonderful, like the oyster shell.

After Mr. Bennie had finished up his story, other men stood and told their own tales one by one. Some were like Mr. Bennie's, others were like sermons, and still others were animal tales. They were serious, boring, scary, or funny, but each storyteller used his own style.

As the last person wound his story down, Jonas could feel his father getting ready to stand up and walk into the circle. If he didn't do something now, it would be too late. He turned to his father, wanting to beg for the chance to tell Grandpa's tale, but his father was already rising to his feet. Quickly Jonas leaped up and stood directly in his father's path.

Everyone grew quiet. His father stopped. He raised his eyebrows at Jonas. "What the matter, son?"

It took Jonas a few seconds to answer. He felt dizzy with fear and embarrassed that everyone was watching. "Please," he finally answered. "I practiced a story and they said I could tell it. Please let me do it. I have to. I want to do it for Grandpa."

His father gave him a hard look. He turned back toward Jonas's mother and Nana Myma. "Let the boy, if he want to," his grandmother answered for them both.

"Go on!" yelled a few of the men, laughing. "Let him give it a try."

Jonas's father turned back to face him. He studied Jonas carefully; then his eyes softened and he nodded. "This my son Jonas, called Oree by some," he said to the crowd. "He gon tell us the tale this evenin'."

Jonas swallowed hard and walked to the front of the crowd. Then into the circle. He fished the lucky coin from his pocket and gripped it in his fist, holding on for all he was worth. He looked around at all the faces, and the words of the story froze on his lips.

Two people pushed to the front of the crowd and waved at him from the side. Zeek and Rikki. He smiled at them and tried to block out everyone else. "Remember the old-time talk," Zeek mouthed at him. Jonas nodded and settled slowly onto the log. Then he began his story in the old Gullah language.

CHAPTER TWELVE

"**B**et lots of you think I too young to remember old Bruh Horse and Bruh Mule," he began, remembering how Nana started her tales.

"You sho' are too young," the crowd answered him.

"Well then," he sassed them, "I gon prove that's not so by tellin' you a tale about 'em."

Everyone laughed. "All right, then go on, tell us!"

"One Sunday noon, the farmer let his plow mule and carriage horse out the pasture together. He give 'em both the day off to rest, and they glad to have the time. Bruh Horse run the field and strut round tossin' his head. He hold his tail out so it stream behind like a willow

branch 'cause he know how pretty it look.

"Bruh Mule trot round the field holdin' his neck out straight as the crow fly. He step high and his tail stand straight up like a thistle. It not such pretty a tail, but it the only one Bruh Mule got and he like it just fine.

"Old Bruh Horse love to brag and show off. 'Look at that pitiful small tuft on the end of your tail,' he say to Bruh Mule. 'Wouldn't you rather have you a beautiful long tail like mine so as you can swish off the fly from biting your skin?' he ask him. 'That sho' is a no-count tail, all right! I a gentleman and you just common,' he told the mule.

"This made Bruh Mule feel shamed. He wasn't satisfied with his tail no more. For true he can't swish flies, but he have thick skin and flies don't bother him no way. Still, Bruh Horse got him feelin' so bad, he forget to tell him that he don't need for swish flies. He just hang his head down and stand off to one side while Bruh Horse play.

"Shortly he noticed a cornfield on the other side of the fence. It an old field that done been harvested, and it full of prickly sheep burrs standin' along with the cornstalks. Bruh Mule get an idea, and he begin to laugh. 'Aw, ee-aw, ee-aw, ee!' he laugh.

"Bruh Horse come runnin' quick. 'What makin' you laugh like that?' he ask him. Bruh Mule tell him he laugh 'cause he don't believe Bruh Horse brave enough to jump the fence and race him through the cornfield.

"Bruh Horse proud, so he take off like a streak and jump that fence. His back foot catch the rail and knock it off, so Bruh Mule tumble over after him. Up and down the cornfield they go, all through them sheep burrs. Bruh Horse runnin' and Bruh Mule trottin'. Bruh Mule tail shaved and slick, 'cept for tuft right on the end, and he swish it round and round in the burrs but none of them stick.

"By and by Bruh Horse tail start to get heavy. That long, silky hair get so full of ol' sheep burrs till it hang stiff and tangly like a rope. Worse of all, every time he swing it round on his back to swish flies, them burrs sting him.

" 'Ouch!' cry Bruh Horse. 'I got spur in my own tail. How I can swish flies now?'

"Bruh Mule pass him by and jump back over the fence to the pasture. He look at old Bruh Horse knotty tail and he not shamed no more of

his own tail. 'Aw, ee-aw, ee-aw, ee!' he laugh. 'Guess it the low tree who left standin' after high winds blow!'

"And that the tale!" he finished.

Jonas looked around at the crowd. He'd done it! He wasn't as good as Grandpa yet, but he had told his story. He had danced around the log, acting out Bruh Horse, just like on the dock, and hadn't even realized it. Everybody was laughing and clapping, and Rikki and Zeek were whooping and stomping their feet!

Jonas almost leaped from the circle back to his seat. Some of the men walked over to his father and patted his back or shook his hand. Jonas could tell his father was proud of him by the way he squeezed the back of Jonas's neck when he sat down. His mother hugged him till he tipped over, but Nana just nodded her head like she always did. "I knew it, fe true," she said. "Oree got de gift fe lie, just like his grandpa."

Jonas's hand was beginning to ache, and he realized he hadn't loosened his grip on the lucky coin since he had begun the tale. He unfolded his stiff fingers and looked at the perfect red circle the metal had pressed into his palm.

His grandpa had left him more than just a lucky coin. He had left Jonas good memories and his family's history through the stories. They were pressed into his mind like the circle on his hand; his forever.

Jonas couldn't do anything about what had happened to Grandpa that morning he died on the dock, but he could do something now. Remember Grandpa and his stories. To forget the stories would let his grandpa down, more than anything else ever could. Jonas didn't need charms or acorn-throwing marsh crows to remind him of that. He only needed to listen to the ones who had known Grandpa best, and that included himself.

AUTHOR'S NOTE

Gullah is a rich and rhythmic creole language spoken by more than a quarter of a million people in the Sea Islands from north Florida to North Carolina. Most who speak it are African American. A creole language is a blend of two or more other languages. Gullah is a blend of West African speech patterns, words, and sounds, and English. It is not broken English, or a dialect, but a true language with regularly recurring patterns. People who speak the English language usually cannot speak or understand the Gullah language.

In this book I used some Gullah phrases and made up a dialect based on Gullah speech rather than write in true Gullah. The following is an example of true Gullah as recorded in the Gullah version of the King James Bible, published by the American Bible Society.

Luke 6:20—"Jedas look at e ciple dem an tell um, say, 'oona bless fa true, oona po people. Cause God esef da rule oba oona!'"

English version—"And he lifted up his eyes on his disciples and said: 'Blessed be ye poor; for yours is the kingdom of God.'"

DATE DUE
